# Last Night I Left Earth for Awhile

### Written & Illustrated by Natalie L. Brown-Douglas

New Voices Publishing

Wilmington, Massachusetts

New Voices Publishing
Wilmington, Massachusetts

For information regarding permission, please write to:
Permissions Department, New Voices Publishing,
P.O. Box 560, Wilmington, Massachusetts, 01887.

Book Design, Typography & Composition by: Arrow Graphics, Inc.
Printed in China

Published by:
New Voices Publishing,
a division of KidsTerrain, Inc.
P.O. Box 560
Wilmington, MA 01887

**Publisher's Cataloging-in-Publication**
***(Provided by Quality Books, Inc.)***

Brown-Douglas, Natalie L.
    Last night I left earth for awhile / written and
illustrated by Natalie L. Brown-Douglas.—1st ed.
    p.  cm.
    SUMMARY: A young child recalls exciting adventures
and marvels at Mother's certainty that, once sleep,
dreams can take you anywhere.
    Audience: Ages 4-8
    LCCN 2001099163
    ISBN: 1-931642-05-2

    1. Dreams—Juvenile fiction. 2. Sleep— Juvenile
fiction. 3. Dreams—Fiction. 4. Sleep— Fiction.
I. Title

PZ8.3.B8175La 2002            [E]
                    QBI02-701325

First Edition:  October 2002
    10 9 8 7 6 5 4 3 2 1

## Dedication

*To my mom and dad
for always tucking me in
&
to Curt and Ethan —
sweet dreams*

Last night I left earth for awhile after my mommy kissed me good night.

"Your dreams can take you anywhere," she said as she tucked me in real tight.

Last night I left earth for awhile and traveled to a far off place.

I flew a shiny rocket
straight into outer space!

I had many adventures
behind my closed eyes.

I dove off a waterfall
a zillion times my size!

I rode high upon an elephant and held on with all my might,

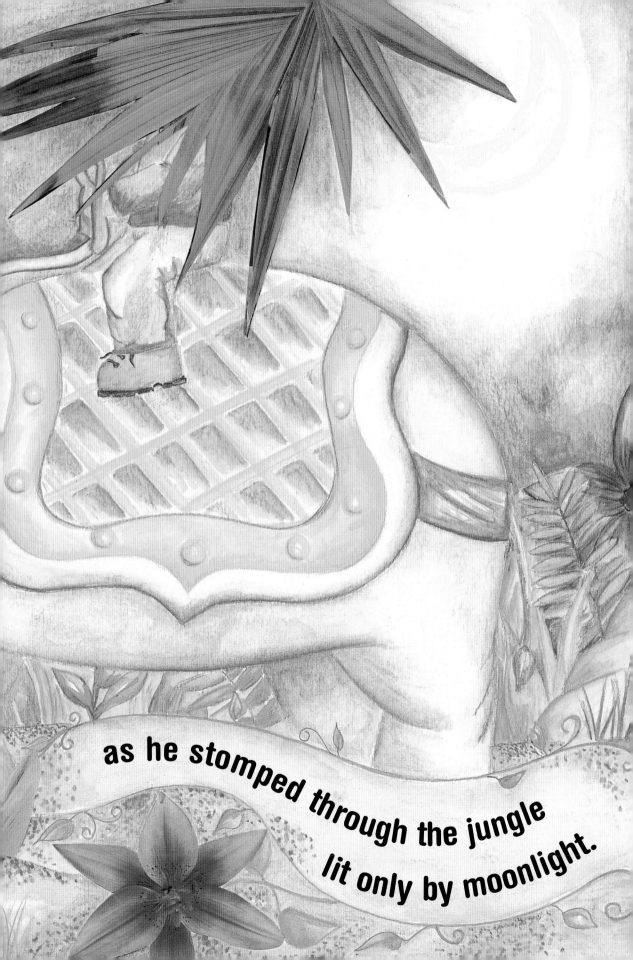

as he stomped through the jungle lit only by moonlight.

I tumbled along with gumballs inside a giant machine.

They popped out in every color — orange, yellow, red, and green!

I swam with some fish
in the deep blue sea,

then was chased by a whale
but he didn't catch me!

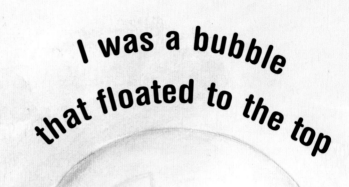

I was a bubble
that floated to the top

I hiked the highest mountain
with a view of every town.

I shouted, "Yippee! Look at me!"
Then wondered, "How will I get down?"

I was a storm cloud who loved to make mud.

But if I let it rain too much, I just might cause a flood!

I spied a fiery dragon, his scales looked like green peas.

He startled me with his roar
and awoke me from my dreams.

"Your dreams can take you anywhere," that's what my mommy said.